WORDS

"A Compilation of Phenomenal Poems"

To: B & B

My Words are now
yours!

10/06

WORDS

"A Compilation of Phenomenal Poems"

Written, edited, published, arranged and designed by:

St. Mark O. Williams

SAINT©

Printed and bound in United Kingdom

CONTENT

Title: **WORDS**

Written by: St. Mark O. Williams

INTRODUCTION

An individual I am who sees more than what my eyes allow. I see with my eyes open and closed, I see with my heart and have the gift to see with the eyes of others; their sights, their tales and with this ability I write from the depth of those convictions. Life and its revelations are continuous pages of poetries and stories to me. People, cultures, love, hate and their passions, nature, birth, death, the changing of time are my gears of motivation. Poetry is ever around me and I find pleasure in grasping words out of the thin air and expressing the occurrences which I have the gift to see and unfold to myself and my fellow human beings who love the sound of life and appreciate it in every manner. For this I now bring you my first self-publish book of poems, with the one thing I have discovered the ability to grasp; I bring to you my very own….. **"WORDS"**.

A book of poems which every reader will embrace, love and have a favourite or two because of my on-the-ball writing skill of expressing real life with the perfect words to be identified and related to. It covers areas of life from our everyday occurrences which is seen and has become such a common sight *(Bus 74)*, to yesterday's news of falling in and out of love and the betrayals of trusted source *(Hypocrite* and *My Forbidden Kin)*. I also cover those happy and glorious moments which are ever so rare *(A Rare Us)* which became stories of our lives giving us *Reason to Love* before becoming *Bitter Sweet.* I acknowledge and value time in *Three Weeks and a Day* describing a love's life span. Sight's powers, our ability to see that ugly is transparent underlining with beauty *(Scarred but Beautiful)*, Earth's matrix of *Human Race, Colours of the World, Circle of Life, A Life's Guide, A perfect Life, Time's Change, All For Nothing* and *Home*(introducing K.E.Williams), Reminiscing with *Memories of Our Fun* and *Hot like Summer* then skimming some of life's dark tales, struggles, wanderings and sufferings with *Narrow Minded, Lonely Soul, Remembering Rita, Ticket To Freedom, Young and Naïve, Tale of A Junkie, Roaming* and *The Greatest Nobody.*
A Book of poems to be loved; revealing issues in life, in death *(R. I. P.)* and showing graciousness to *God.*
                              St. Mark O. Williams

St. Mark O. Williams' Poetry

"WORDS NOT TAKEN LIGHTLY"

WORDS

By St. Mark O. Williams

Words are often spoken at various levels in life
Expressing emotions of love, anger and strife
It is foundation of the basic conversation
It is the cause and likewise the remedy for most frustration
Uttered or unuttered, words are being said
Words... Those little voices we always hear in our heads
It is the captain when we are making up our minds
Words... the cause of my first smiles; hearing nursery rhymes
Words has been all the lessons that I've learnt
Words...a life filled with it, is a life well earned.

WORDS

"A Compilation Of Phenomenal Poems"

Three Weeks & A Day

By St. Mark O. Williams

A chance I took to say hi
Being normally shy
The response was positive
An obvious no-regret for what I did
Acquaintances we instantly became
A rare happiness was discovered aboard a train
Curiosity and crave had gotten the best of us
As we phoned, sent texts and emails; we kept in touch
A fight with nature we had, trying to slow our pace
Making it seem that intimacy could wait
Our bodies yearn as our personalities lied
The truth… the two of us wanting to hide
For her, it was the sake of being morally decent
For me, a true gentleman with a pure difference
But then we embraced and breathe in each others face
Second thoughts were late, we had erupted an earthquake
With the gushing, burning flow of lava
This got intense with in-pours of perspiration and saliva
But constancy eventually made it calm
And then she was gone
Disappear!
As if she was never here
Shock disturbed me mentally
As I refused to accept the reality
A lifetime with her had came my way
And ended precisely in *three weeks and a day.*

WORDS

"A Compilation Of Phenomenal Poems"

Cheating Heart

By St. Mark O. Williams

Even though I had the evidence to prove her guilt
Firm was how she stood on her lies and wouldn't tilt
With marks of passion on her neck and aftershave scented sheet
Was more than enough to prove that my angel was a cheat
But still she denied; saying that my facts were lies
And how dare I accuse her of being with another guy
"But I called you on the phone, didn't you hear it ring?"
"You couldn't have, she said, I didn't hear a thing!"
"I also knocked at the door and saw the silhouettes moved."
"Stop it!" she shouted. "I'll take no more of this abuse."
Beautiful it was at first, seemingly the perfect match
And as it ended, we both had perfect reasons to detach.

WORDS

"A Compilation Of Phenomenal Poems"

A Rare "Us"

By St. Mark O. Williams

Happy times are here
Even though it comes with fear
Two of a kind is clear
Worried hearts hope it won't disappear
Little faith we have in dreams
Happiness came and went too many times; our lives' routine
Our hearts have had their share of rise and fall
And our eyes have practically seen it all
People of our statues have circled the block
In slang, "been there, done that!"
But "us"! What about us?
No dislikes, no arguments, no fuss?
Feels great, unusual and strange
Is this real; has our lives' routines change?
Overwhelmed I am with the whole you
Your talks, your walk, just to name a few
If this is a dream, there's one thing I ask
Don't wake me; I want this one to last.

WORDS

"A Compilation Of Phenomenal Poems"

Love's Price

By St. Mark O. Williams

In my heart I truly want it
Ideal for me it is, a perfect fit
But a price is there, a cost, a fee
A reminder that nothing's for free
Although it's nice and worth twice the price
So much to pay; the ultimate sacrifice
To share, to adjust, to edit my standard
I've pushed myself before, but never this hard
For smiles and bliss with some down times
I am paying in full and willing to sign the dotted line.

WORDS

"A Compilation Of Phenomenal Poems"

Narrow-Minded

By St. Mark O. Williams

A dark tunnel, a passage of doom
Lights ahead! Won't be seen soon
Adjustment to the dark eventually came
An illusion which now controls the brain
Deceiving you as sight when there's no light
Seeing a clear image when none of it is vivid
Subconscious speaks the truth
Gets treated as mute
Fear of change or comfort in the dark
Has put you and most of the world far apart
Stuck in the mud, stooped in the dark, refusing to move
A man's destiny; the way of life he choose.

WORDS

"A Compilation Of Phenomenal Poems"

Home

By K.E. Williams

I am where serenity lies
Where dreams and promises rise
Comfort I shall give to you
Blessings all year through
Peace and joy for evermore
At the openings and closings of my door
Around the world you may roam
And still find no other place like home.

WORDS

"A Compilation Of Phenomenal Poems"

Human Race

By St. Mark O. Williams

Life. A racetrack with its dreaded finish lines
Awaiting our arrivals, yours and mine
Randomly life selects who should finish
But to stay in this race is everyone's wish
Reaching the finish line is terribly feared
Everyone who has reached it, just disappeared
Vanish, without a trace
No wonder the goal is to prolong this race
Giving it your best run, clean and fair
Running a few more miles, but the finish is still near
The track is a circle; the line can't be missed
Sooner or later, we will have to reach it.

WORDS

"A Compilation Of Phenomenal Poems"

Scarred But Beautiful

By St. Mark O. Williams

Your eyes, I see so much beauty in them
Though your appearance doesn't attract many friends
You lack grace in your walk and you move in doubt
Wondering if in every whisper you are being talked about
Being criticized for only exposing your eyes
But still a body where a good heart lies
Give me those eyes; let me be your mirror
To see your body and all through the horror
Undress for me and free your tears
Let me kiss your burn marks and rid your fears
Take my eyes in return and see what I see
No scars, no burn, nothing that is ugly
But a human who's got so much to give
A human with so much more reasons to live.

WORDS

"A Compilation Of Phenomenal Poems"

Bus 74

By St. Mark O. Williams

Every morning I get on that bus, at 15 pass 5
And even though I'm on just for an eleven minutes ride
Its predictable of who I will see inside
The same faces. Two ladies and twenty-five guys
Such a wide selection to write on
But only a few I'll mention
Starting with that black guy who sits in the back
With twisted-hair; my guess, a wannabe dreadlocks
One of the ladies gets off at the very next stop
All the guys stares at her; making their cool morning hot
Upfront a white guy with a racist symbol tattooed to his head
No wonder he sits so far from the dread
A few stops up, this fella will come on
Sleep still in his eyes and greets the crew with a yawn
Across from me, a 70s style dressed guy, in a world of his own
Always bopping away to the sounds of his ear phones
The next stop another guy will come on, looking stressed, early as it is
Makes you kinda wonder who he woke up with
Then there's this weird guy (me) with paper and pen
Looking crazy in thoughts staring at them
Next stop is mine and I'm out the door
Tomorrow I'll see it again on bus 74

WORDS

"A Compilation Of Phenomenal Poems"

Lonely Soul

By St. Mark O. Williams

Born into this world and abandoned at twelve
Harsh reality taught him to depend on himself
Alone but never lonely
At home but never homely
No brothers, no sisters, no family ties
Here today, gone tomorrow, but still under these skies

WORDS

"A Compilation Of Phenomenal Poems"

Circle Of Life

By St. Mark O. Williams

A year starts, a year ends
Then it will all happen again
A rotation of nights and days
A historic era, a doubtful phase
A time when so many things may happen
Never knowing to whom, where nor when
Some will laugh, some will cry, and most will do the two
Some...some... Could be me, could be you
Geared for the worst, hoping for delight
The goal: Make it through another day and survive another night

WORDS

"A Compilation Of Phenomenal Poems"

Never Giving Up

By St. Mark O. Williams

Believing in myself took me half-way there
Being pushed by a helping hand could make my mist clear
A leap into the winner's circle
Around the bend and over the hurdles
Straight to the top spot for the sake of *never giving up*
Achieving rewards for my ability rather than luck.

WORDS

"A Compilation Of Phenomenal Poems"

Hypocrite

By St. Mark O. Williams

Smiles you express to me, though your heart despise
Far from being genuine, your whole image is a lie
Wishing the best, when in truth you desire a wreck
My accomplishment of failures have been your success
You extend compliments, but the sight you resent
Saying kind words which you never really meant
Your philosophy deals in hypocrisy
Your words sound full, but their meanings are empty
A user you are too, of everyone else
Exploitation got the best of you, you now use yourself
Just to get ahead and shine above the rest
You will do anything, even if it makes your life a mess
With hypocrisy and selfishness; the ways you live
Is it a puzzle that I class you as self-destructive?

WORDS

"A Compilation Of Phenomenal Poems"

Time's Change

By St. Mark ☉. Williams

I can remember a simple phase
More relaxing, laid-back and longer days
A time when everything didn't move so fast
And my body didn't know exhaust
But now everything's change
Life has gotten strange
A new era of "Technological Increase"
Modern adaptation; the ridding of antiques
Good or bad, it is what it is
A change in our time we now have to live with
Question: a change to embrace or a change to fear?
Benefits: better cars, better homes, better TV's, better nuclear.

WORDS

"A Compilation Of Phenomenal Poems"

All for Nothing

By St. Mark O. Williams

Life: A stage of controversial topics
Results into confusion, stemming from endless gossips
Speculations of what is, was and could be
Regarding the current time and history
Different opinions, a common reason for feud
Servings of bombshell and deprivation of food
Man: a strange creature, aiming to rid its own kind
A seemingly chosen hobby used to pass time
Egoistic, power-gluttons competing in vain
For fruitless reward and recognition and fame.

WORDS

"A Compilation Of Phenomenal Poems"

Colours of the World

By St. Mark O. Williams

Racism: a poor excuse for hate
Ignorant humans continue to discriminate
Of what was intended to be beauty of the world
One colour is being desired with no added swirl
Black people united against white
An obvious few who are far from being bright
Skin-heads, K.K.K. or the National Front
Are organized hate-groups; qualification: Dunce
Hating for the colour of skin
Where and when did this madness begin?
Colour-envy or colour-hate
A bunch of sleeping heads who needs to be awake
And learn that all man are equally created by god
We all deserve to be here and none of us are odd

WORDS

"A Compilation Of Phenomenal Poems"

Reasons to Love

By St. Mark O. Williams

The reasons why I love you and the obvious truth:
You have been my life-long companion and shared years of my youth
Such a long time you and I have been together
Side by side, hand in hand, been through the weathers
You are my everything; my days and my nights
Who shared my glories and fought my fights
My sunshine and my rain
You shared my laughs and suffered my pains
Through my ups and my downs
Your support is consistent and never with a frown
You have dedicated your entire life to mine
And vowed to love me 'til the end of time
Nothing is ever too much for you to do for me
I dedicate my life and my love to you for eternity
You are the greatest gift a man could have in his life
And grateful I am to have you for my wife.

I love you, Sweetheart!

WORDS

"A Compilation Of Phenomenal Poems"

Remembering Rita

By St. Mark O. Williams

A seemingly average human being
But up close and personal, she is not of the theme
An introduction of the norm brought her into my world
My first impression of her: an average, kind and charming girl
Who offered gifts and accepts no rejections
But that kindness turns out to be quite a deception
For all the cheap gifts she bought
She expects a repayment of the ultimate cost
To rule over my life and do everything she says
Forget everything I know and live the Rita's way
But I refused and her feelings got bruised
Instantly I became a bearer of bad news
With a proposal to cut all ties
Not cruel nor kind, but an understanding good-bye
The actions taken thereafter, I guess it has its reason
I was iron-clad and Rita had to get even
She conjured a string of false allegations
This made me subject to hours of interrogation
Fruitless fibs which wouldn't stick onto a shelf
I remember Rita at times and wonder how she lives with herself.

WORDS

"A Compilation Of Phenomenal Poems"

God

By St. Mark O. Williams

You have always been my guide and my saviour indeed
You always being my refuge in times of need
Never letting me down; always here when I call
Whether my troubles are big and massive or meager and small
A reward I receive for the way I lead my life
Proud to see that in my thoughts you have found delight
In your reward I have found the same
When my enemies make me a target, they always miss their aims
Your actions are wonderful sights to behold
And you have made my life a beautiful story to be told
My guide, my defence, my supporting rod
No one deserves this credit more than you, my friend, my father, my god.

WORDS

"A Compilation Of Phenomenal Poems"

Smoke Gets In Your Eyes

By St. Mark ☉. Williams

Disappeared from your view, though none of it is true
Habbra Kaddabra! This magician says to you
Took control of your imagination and presented an illusion
Having you believe what is said and done
The magician shoots him dead, with no bullet in the gun
But for you, he is dead because that's what was said
And you should have no other thoughts in your head
Think nothing of the cloud of smoke blown in your eyes
The sound of the gun is real and the man on the floor has died
The truth, a con, a trick, a fib?
Speculate if you want, but no one must know that he lives.

WORDS

"A Compilation Of Phenomenal Poems"

Tale of The Endless Scroll

By St. Mark O. Williams

Dreams and desires of human beings growing old
From trials and efforts, their skins are scarred and mould
Success brought warmth and joy, failures brought bitterness and cold
Accomplished or failed, there's always another goal
Writing seem to exist on every unfold
Is it destined or are we the ones lengthening this scroll?

WORDS

"A Compilation Of Phenomenal Poems"

My Forbidden Kin

By St. Mark O. Williams

Relatives linked together by blood
Share the same mother, received the same love
A family we were, mom's own little team
She said, "Look out for each other, let nothing come between."
An advice to strengthen us being family and friends
Like an army defending each other to the end
And today we are at WAR
One of our soldiers is down, wounded and scarred
A rebel against the perpetrator should be a must
But in this case, the perpetrator is also one of us
Ambushed by you, our very own brother
You betrayed our team and resented Mother
Now we are forced to see you as the enemy
No longer can you be considered family
Sticking as a team, if we lose or win
And you to us are just "The Forbidden Kin"

WORDS

"A Compilation Of Phenomenal Poems"

Who Are You?

By St. Mark O. Williams

Who are you?
No! My question really is: Who am I to you?
A friend! No, not a friend
Let's try again.

Who are you? I mean, who am I to you?
I guess if "friend" isn't the answer, then you haven't got a clue.

Recently I looked at myself using your eyes
And the things I saw was quite a surprise
I saw myself as a money machine and a charity shop
Only when in need, you ever bothered to stop
I saw that my car was your personal free ride
And that those are the only times we sat side by side

The worst thing I saw was: *"A fool I am, take all I have"*
a sign posted on my door
My address had no number, it just says, *"convenient store"*

Now, if you should ask, who am I to you? I would never say friend
What I'm saying is, *"The store is close, please don't come again"*.

WORDS

"A Compilation Of Phenomenal Poems"

My dog, THUGG

By St. Mark O. Williams

There are times when you get on my nerves
And at those moments I wished I'd gotten birds
But it'd be no good to me having my pet in a cage
Locked up and chirping away all day
Besides, I love you too much
The wagging of your tail and your woof-woofs
Not to have you around now would leave such an empty space
Which no other cute or cuddly dog could replace
It shows how bonded we are when I take you on your walks
And especially the way we play *"fetch the ball"* at the park
The excitement you possess each time I walk through the door
Jumping up and down, bouncing off the floor
Your loyalty is clear and if necessary ready to defend
You have displayed living-proof to the slogan: *"Man's Best Friend"*.

WORDS

"A Compilation Of Phenomenal Poems"

A Perfect Life

By St. Mark Θ. Williams

Some of us take the time out to format our lives
To have the kids, the income and the wife
Thereafter, take life for what it is; one day at a time
Falls into that routine and everything is fine
That format will one day be interrupted by death
But a well lived life for some; awesome. Perfect.

WORDS

"A Compilation Of Phenomenal Poems"

Dead Man Talking

By St. Mark O. Williams

Though thoughts of you vaguely linger in my head
I am walking, I am talking, but really I am dead
Moved on it seem and found someone new
But lifeless I am without the energy of you
Trying to re-live and adjust to a new life
But bright, sunny days are just the darkest, starless nights
No torches, no candles to add the tiniest spark
No whispers of hope, no kind remark
My hand longing to hold another, I feel alone
A house I have, but longing for a home
Loneliness targeted me and has commenced its stalking
I am drained and what you are listening to is a *"dead man talking"*.

WORDS

"A Compilation Of Phenomenal Poems"

Tale of A Junkie

By St. Mark ☉. Williams

To reach our goals require strength, but I am not strong
And the route I alternate is obviously wrong
An inner voice screamed, Give up! Abort!
Now I smoke, I drink and I snort
Controlled substance
Sending me to a distant
Away from life's harsh struggles
But in reality, I just doubled my troubles
Trying to rid one struggle I created a next
I thought my life was hard before, but it just got complex
I am an addict!
A penniless bum who can't support his habits
And though my life was complex, it got even worst
Desperate for my fix, I stole an old lady's purse
Now a fugitive!
A penniless, on-the-run drug addict, with nowhere to live
"Give up! Abort!" says the voice in my head
"But to get back to life's struggle, the route is now a cell's bed".

WORDS

"A Compilation Of Phenomenal Poems"

Fear

By St. Mark O. Williams

Fear. The emotion that rules when we are scared
And our sixth sense says danger nears
It's when we are afraid
Happiness and joy skipped our days
Uncertain! Not sure!
Of what's behind the door
Curious of a sound
The heart races and pound
A feeling we dread
And want out of our heads.

WORDS

"A Compilation Of Phenomenal Poems"

Young and Naïve

By St. Mark O. Williams

Young and naïve, ready for mould
Could be a distinguished gentleman or a hoodlum out-of-control
Two signs lay ahead, but which will he choose
One's sign-posted "win" and the other is sign-posted "lose"
But the route "lose" seem so attractive
And "win" looks so plain
Young and naïve he is and thought someone must've switched names
So he chose "lose"
And learnt that the attraction was a disguise for bad news
Years to come he suffered and ached
Grew old being haunted by his mistake
Everything captured by sight, he learnt not to believe
He soothes his aches and pains by saying he was just "young and naïve".

WORDS

"A Compilation Of Phenomenal Poems"

Ticket to Freedom

By St. Mark Θ. Williams

The world is against me, that's how it seemed
Locked away, sentenced to life, an outcast human being
Injustice is my claim
A successful conspiracy added flaws to my name
But am I innocent? Questions are yet to face
Do I truly deserve to be apart of freedom's space?
After all, I did commit an awful crime
Should it be overlooked as if everything is fine?

Being honest to myself I thought on what I'd done
Then I realize that an appeal was not my ticket to freedom
Nor would it be any legal proceedings in the courts
It was acceptance of my guilt and genuine remorse
I said to myself, I have performed an evil act
I felt the pain I once inflicted and wished I could take it back
I became a new man and released my inner-child
Exhaled, away with anger and welcomed gentle, meek and mild
A task I set for myself, to let my blind side flee
I accomplished it and in more ways than one, I was then set free.

31.

WORDS

"A Compilation Of Phenomenal Poems"

Roaming

By St. Mark O. Williams

I move from cities to cities and from towns to towns
On God's grace is how I get around
With no set plans nor destinations
I set off from airports and bus stations
No dependents and no family ties
Off I go down the highways or across the blue skies
In this odyssey, I meet so many and become apart of their lives
I even had phases with step-children and have had common-law wives
Made homes, had jobs, tried to bound my feet
But a drive in me always sends me on my beat
Roaming, gone again to relocate
A tumble-weed in the wind or simply my fate?

WORDS

"A Compilation Of Phenomenal Poems"

The Greatest Nobody

By St. Mark O. Williams

I'm **the greatest**…though I never had fans screaming my name
I am **the greatest** even though there's no mention of me in the roll-call of fame
No one thinks much of my photographs
Still, I am **the greatest**, though no one needs my autograph.

Never act in Hollywood, never played Pro
To them I am nobody as far as it goes
I've never been broadcast or ever played a sport
I've never been in parliament and I never ruled in court

But I am **the greatest**, I've beat their best
I have taken bad photographs and had no distress
I go about as I please with no need for a bodyguard
Freedom as I stroll, such a sweet reward
And when I sign, it's my purchase receipt at the till
No fear of being abducted, they know I don't have a mil

My home-made videos are priceless, so priceless, there's only one copy
Another rich reward for being **The Greatest Nobody**.

WORDS

"A Compilation Of Phenomenal Poems"

Memories of our fun

By St. Mark Θ. Williams

Funny, but I knew that this day would come
When I would stare in space and sigh on our segments of fun
I knew that we had to part and set each other free
Little things were evidence that we weren't meant to be
And before we parted I knew that you would be missed
Future days like today, I knew I would reminisce
On the percentages of fun we share
On the warm, cuddly times when you were near
I was sure to miss that little part, which made us compatible
That little sign of hope that made forever seem possible
But the greater part always hurt my feelings
The truth of us not lasting kept revealing
The day we parted, what had to be was done
But what cuddles and still keeps me warm are **memories of our fun.**

WORDS

"A Compilation Of Phenomenal Poems"

Before You Were My Wife

By St. Mark O. Williams

Before you were my wife, you were my best friend
Whenever I was in need, on you could depend
Before you were my wife, you were my guide
In good times and bad, you were by my side
Before you were my wife, you were my other mother
When no one else would hear me out, you I could bother
Before you were my wife, you accepted all my faults
And told me that all my ways are stored in your heart's vault
Before you were my wife, I knew that one day you would be
Ever since I fell for you, I wanted to say, marry me
You are the true reason why I pursue life
You added so much value to my world, *before you were my wife.*

WORDS

"A Compilation Of Phenomenal Poems"

Hot Like Summer

By St. Mark O. Williams

These past few nights has been outrageously hot
It's no use checking the temperature on the thermostat
Sleeping, the sheet moves from dampness to wet
That's how much this Summer's heat causes me to sweat
But thank goodness, August is coming to an end
And September will soon be here starting a cooler trend
I love Summer, allowing outdoor activities and all
But the way this one turned up its heat, I most welcome this Fall.

WORDS

"A Compilation Of Phenomenal Poems"

Bitter Sweet

By St. Mark O. Williams

Exciting it was, I got swept right off my feet
The way you use to look at me and drown me with your
treats
The phone calls were overwhelming, but nothing compared to our
dates
My admiration grew high for your attitude of never being late
Our kisses were long and obviously sweet
Happy you would appear every single time we meet
Silly you would act, singing and reciting love verses
And always reminding me of how much I was worth it
How I hoped that you would always be the same
Now I guess that all my hopes were just hopes in vain
Because look at us now
This is not the way for lovers to grow.

After the marriage and the children, everything just got strange
The way you use to look at me has definitely changed
And it's not for the better; it has changed for the worse
No more dates, no more treats and no more love verse
Our kisses now gapped more than twenty-four hours
And I'm almost sure that the taste of them now would be sour
We've worked so hard, so long we've sweat
I'm ready to work hard again to make it like when
we first met

WORDS

"A Compilation Of Phenomenal Poems"

A True Love Story
(A dedication to Kamilia E. Black)

By St. Mark O. Williams

We've known each other ever since we were kids
You shared the same neighbourhood where I once lived
It wasn't intimidation, but I don't know why
The most I remembered ever saying to you was just 'hi'
Besides I was about five or six years older than you was
It would've been a remote thought to think that we would ever be in love
But years later that's how it turned out to be
That kid I barely noticed now means the world to me
Our life seem like something of a cast
Ironic, but funny it is when we reflect on our past
Never kissed, never hugged and never saw a sign
Never thought for a second that you would ever be mine
The way our lives turned out is still a mystery
But proud we are about its entire history
Happy and in love is as good as it gets
You and I categorized as Romeo and Juliet.

WORDS

"A Compilation Of Phenomenal Poems"

R. I. P.
(In memory of David "Dice" Simpson)

By St. Mark ☉. Williams

It happened so fast, I mean before any of them could warn
He was hit off his bike and just like that; he was gone
At the hands of a reckless driver who didn't bother to stop
But sped on instead
Leaving behind; *David Simpson* dead
It came as a shock when I heard the news
Hoping he would have just suffered broken bones or just a bruise
As it turned out, it wasn't so
He's dead, deceased, gone; oh, no!

You are no longer around, my friend
I just have to face it; your journey came to its end
But the times we have shared, I will never forget
Your absence has put more meaning to when we first met
In your time, together we laughed, grieved, drank and *man*, we could eat
For all those times, it hurts to say this, but I must; **REST IN PEACE.**

WORDS

"A Compilation Of Phenomenal Poems"

My Love For You

By St. Mark O. Williams

Sometimes I ask myself, why do I love thee
Then I realize that the answers aren't just within me
But rather, they have much to do with you
Most of it may seem strange, but all of it is true
How at times you can be so stubborn and make me so mad
Speak of my flaws and make me feel so bad
And at other times you would express your undying love
Of wanting to shower me with your kisses and hugs
Good or bad, you always tell me how you feel
I admires that and classifies it as being "real"
Our love is of a rare kind, and somewhat a mystery
At times I think our love should go down in history
Of how you and I fell in love and exchange our hearts
People should forget about Romeo and Juliet and read about you
and St. Mark
Because we aren't just lovers nor we just friends
We are *"Lovers for life"* and *"Friends to the end"*
We are ordinary human beings who argues and fuss
But our disputes never affect our love nor our trust
You are everything I ever wanted in a woman
There's no need adding to you nor making subtractions
I was lucky that day when you walked into my life
And I'm blessed with the fact that you are now my wife
You were just as lucky when I entered your life too
And you are blessed because I'll always love you.

WORDS

"A Compilation Of Phenomenal Poems"

A Poet's Loss
(In memory of Ron J. Emler)

By St. Mark O. Williams

I am a poet, a man of words
Most of what is recited, you have already heard
Now speechless though thoughts are in my head
No reply I gave to what you just said
The news you gave
The mention of a grave
My Father so brave
Should have been a close shave
My strength, my life
The reason I write
My friend
My pen
Never a need to think
He was the words that form from my ink
Now gone
Left me alone
But with a memory
our history
Enough to write more short stories.

WORDS

"A Compilation Of Phenomenal Poems"

A Life's Guide

Inspirational advice by St. Mark O. Williams © 2001

With love and full intention that people may grasp Knowledge, Wisdom, Understanding and that they may Value all that life possess to them as long as they may live in this thing we all call LIFE.

Life is strict and full of discipline, its mainstream is "time", which never stops, pauses nor turn back for anyone nor anything. Life is what you as an individual make it to be and so is each moment of it. You are ruler of your life and believe it when I say; all of your life's results are outcomes of your own governing. In life we receive gifts of all nature and aspects from others expressing said and unsaid feelings; though most gifts are purchased, it is wise to value gifts as priceless, not for sale or exchange. We are all we've got in this life (people and each other). Never take people for granted, especially the ones we hold as most dear; understand that life is short and memories and gifts will soon be the only page of reflection we can go through. Death is a great part of life and should never be ignored, no matter how long it seems we have lived, our time alive is temporary. Realize your existence that you are human, made from a merciful and peaceful God. A watchful eye is forever on us…live good! Know that evil and corruption are ever surrounding us; you have a free will to participate therein or refrain thereof. The good, the bad and the indifferent occurrences, they all have their purposes; take a lesson from them. Value love, people (the gifts they give, the works they do and their existence), value words and most of all, value life, from the very air that you breathe and everything that follows. Be wise in all your doings.

WORDS

"A Compilation Of Phenomenal Poems"

Acknowledgement

My thanks and appreciation is being extended to the following people for their support and aspirations given to me in my goal to become a published writer:

Ruby D. Gibbs (USA), Kamilia E. Black-Williams, Kevon Seigler (USA), Pamela Seigler (USA), Cory Madison Williams (USA), Martina Madison (USA), Ronald Emler (USA), Charlotte Hill (USA), Kenneth Bagley (USA), Jesus Avila, Basil Harper (USA), Kennesha Richards(JA), Jennifer Wint (UK), Dawn Manning (UK), Charmaine Carpenter (UK), Allan Johnson, Sajeen Bell, Hope Mullings (UK), Kevin Lawrence (USA), Kalvin Lawrence (USA), Starskey Ivey (USA) and Birmingham Central Library (UK).

This book is dedicated to:

Mr. Ronald J. Emler, author of 'The Ghost of Echo Park©'
Founder of Echo Park Security Association
Co-founder of Echo Park Improvement Association
Co-founder of Echo Park Historical Society
and
my mentor.

'The Ghost of Echo Park©' who lives on in our hearts forever.

THE END.